Jacques Prévert

How to Paint
the Portrait
of a Bird

Illustrations and Translation by
Mordicai Gerstein

Roaring Brook Press
New York

First paint a cage

with an open door.

Then, in the cage, paint something for the bird,

something useful and beautiful, but simple.

Then take the picture to a garden

. . . or a park

. . . or a forest.

Put the picture under a tree.
Hide behind the tree.

Don't speak.
Don't move.

Sometimes the bird comes quickly.
But it can just as well take years before deciding.

If the bird doesn't come right away,
don't be discouraged. Wait.

Wait years if necessary.

It doesn't mean that your picture won't be good.

When the bird comes, if it comes,

remain absolutely silent.

Wait till the bird enters the cage.

Then gently close the door with your brush.

Then,

erase the cage, one bar at a time,
being very careful of the bird's feathers.

Now paint the portrait of the tree

with the prettiest branch for the bird.

Paint the green leaves and the summer breeze.

Paint the smell of the sunshine and the flowers,
and the songs of the bees and the butterflies.

Then wait for the bird to sing.

If it doesn't sing, don't be sad.
You did your best.

But if the bird sings,

it's a very good sign.

It's a sign that you can sign.
So then, *very* gently, take a feather from the bird
and write your name in a corner of the picture.

(Tomorrow you can paint another one.)

For
Aram, Marina,
Daisy and Hugh
with all my
love.
—M.G.

"Pour faire le portrait d'un oiseau" by Jacques Prévert © Editions GALLIMARD, Paris, 1949.
Translation and illustrations copyright © 2007 by Mordicai Gerstein.
Published by Roaring Brook Press
Roaring Brook Press is a division of Holtzbrinck Publishing Holdings Limited Partnership
175 Fifth Avenue, New York, NY 10010
www.roaringbrookpress.com

Distributed in Canada by H. B. Fenn and Company Ltd.

Library of Congress Cataloging-in-Publication Data
Prévert, Jacques, 1900-1977.
[Pour faire le portrait d'un oiseau. English]
To paint the portrait of a bird / by Jacques Prévert ; translated and illustrated by Mordicai Gerstein.
p. cm.
ISBN-13: 978-1-59643-215-4
ISBN-10: 1-59643-215-2
1. Children's poetry, French. I. Gerstein, Mordicai, ill. II. Title.
PQ2631.R387P68 2007
841'.914--dc22
2006032183

Roaring Brook Press books are available for special promotions and premiums.
For details contact: Director of Special Markets, Holtzbrinck Publishers.

First Edition September 2007
Book design by Filomena Tuosto
Printed in the United States of America
1 3 5 7 9 10 8 6 4 2